THE WHITE HOUSE

Dec 2018

THE WHITE HOUSE

BY JAQUAVIS COLEMAN

Infamous

Published by Akashic Books
©2014 JaQuavis Coleman

Hardcover ISBN-13: 978-1-61775-262-9
Paperback ISBN-13: 978-1-61775-261-2
Library of Congress Control Number: 2013956780

Infamous Books
www.infamousbooks.net

Akashic Books
Twitter: @AkashicBooks
Facebook: AkashicBooks
E-mail: info@akashicbooks.com
Website: www.akashicbooks.com

Also available from Infamous Books

Black Lotus
by K'wan

Swing
by Miasha

H.N.I.C.
by Albert "Prodigy" Johnson with Steven Savile

Ritual
by Albert "Prodigy" Johnson and Steven Savile
(forthcoming)

AUTHOR'S NOTE

Hello All,

Writing this story was very important to me. I wanted to give a lesson on karma and life ills while holding your attention. I intentionally drop subtle gems for the people like me who came from where I came. There are always two layers to my books; not everyone will get the second layer but the ones who do . . . they feel me. You see, I talk to the readers but I whisper to the streets. The streets being people who grew up in the struggle and love to read books because it closely resembles their current or past lifestyles. My books are conversational or at least that's what my intentions are.

If you ever prayed to God, asking Him to show you the way, but in the same breath asking for forgiveness for the things you may have to do until you see the light . . . this one is for you. I understand. I am you . . . you are me. I am the streets. Love you all. *Raises cigar*

—*JaQuavis Coleman*

PROLOGUE

DRAYA ARCHED HER BACK IN PURE PLEASURE as she dug her nails deep into the man's chocolate muscular back. He slowly ground his hips in circular motions as he dove deep inside of her leaking love box. His swollen testicles gently slapped against her other entry with each thrust. Splashing noises echoed throughout the room, accompanied by Draya's light moans and cries. Their sweaty bodies bounced off each other as the man began to whisper in her ear. The hot summer night made the air moist and their bodies seemed to glow as the moon's light crept through the blinds and reflected off of them.

"You're always going to be mine. I missed you, baby girl," he said as he dug even deeper, rubbing her hair while he sexed her.

Draya hadn't felt him in over a year and she almost forgot how good of a stroke he had. She began to pant heavily and her legs started to shake. First it was small quivers, then it grew to vigorous and sporadic jerking spasms. She felt a gigantic orgasm approaching and her body began to tense up. The man, with precision, sped up his stroke and quickly put his hands under her cheeks and spread them wider. Draya was in complete heaven as she felt his warm hands gently squeezing her plump buttocks. She tried to tell him how good it was, but she couldn't talk because she was on the brink of exploding all over him. She felt his thickness fill her up with each thrust and it seemed as if his pole was on fire . . . it was so hot. The feeling was driving Draya crazy; a good crazy though. He stroked the long way, pulling his whole shaft out of her, leaving only the very tip of it in before he plunged it all the way back in. He was putting on a masterful performance that night.

"Oooh," she crooned as she squeezed him tighter, feeling her climax beginning. The man, with perfect timing, pulled out and dipped down, placing his mouth on her love box and catching everything she squirted out. Draya's legs quivered as she released her juices onto his face and into his mouth. She shook uncontrollably when she gripped the back of his head, almost pile-driving his face into herself. Her body jerked violently as he continued to give her clitoris an oral massage. The man then rose up and slid back into her. It didn't take long for him to release a load into her. Draya didn't care if he came inside of her; he felt too good. She remembered at that moment that she once loved him, but she had let greed get in the way of that.

"I missed you. I missed you so much," the man whispered in her ear, resting on top of her, breathing heavily as his sweat dripped onto her body. His deep baritone sent chills down Draya's spine and she wondered why she had ever stopped messing with him in the first place.

"Oh . . . oh my God. That was so good," Draya professed as he placed her hand on her love box and added pressure. It was so tender and sore . . . a pleasant sore. It hurt so badly, but then again, it felt so good. The man kissed her on the forehead softly and got up from the king-size bed. He headed to the hotel suite's bathroom while Draya's eyes admired his physique. His chiseled back and muscular frame instantly made her want him again. The man disappeared into the bathroom and Draya flipped over onto her stomach and ran her fingers through her sweated-out hair. She took a deep breath and smiled.

"You were amazing, Daddy. I am so glad I ran into you." She looked around the luxury suite and noticed a slightly opened duffel bag sitting on the floor. She could just glimpse some plastic-wrapped cocaine bricks stacked neatly inside of it and she chuckled to herself.

"I see not a lot has changed since the last time I saw you. You still getting it in, huh?" she said as she sat up and began tying her hair into a ponytail.

"You know it, Ma. Don't shit stop," he called back as he turned on the faucet.

Draya smiled and thought back on how she had robbed him blind a year earlier and he never knew a thing. She had set him up so smoothly and disappeared from town like a ghost. He had no idea that his biggest loss came from a chick who he had love for. She kept chuckling to herself while shaking her head with regret.

That's the way the game goes sometimes. I had to get mine, she thought, trying to make herself feel better about what she'd done. *If a nigga get caught slipping, it's his own fault.*

She flipped onto her stomach and grabbed her phone from the nightstand. As she began to scroll through her contacts, she heard the water turn off and then the footsteps of the man approaching her. She wiggled her plump butt cheeks, knowing that he was watching, and smiled and giggled while still focusing on her phone.

She felt his warm hands begin to rub on her back and then heard his deep voice: "It's been a long time, baby." He took her phone from her and set it aside, then gently pulled her hands behind her back. His demand for her attention turned Draya on and made her smile even wider. She could feel his growing warm shaft resting on her leg. That sensation alone made her clitoris begin to jump in anticipation of round two. She started moving her body like a snake, in a circular motion, causing friction between the bed and her clitoris as she closed her eyes in total bliss. With her arms still behind her back, it made everything more exotic and she was loving every second of it.

"Please put it in again, Daddy," she begged, and frowned up in pleasure.

The man remained silent and prepared to give her the business. The cold handcuffs startled Draya as they were slapped across her wrists. Almost instantly, a bandanna was slipped between her lips and he tied it behind her head so tightly that it hurt.

"I've been waiting to catch you for over a year, you grimy bitch," he said as Draya began to squirm like a wet fish. It all happened so fast that she hadn't seen it coming. Something crashed down on the back of her skull, causing her whole world to shake up. Her vision went blurry and the most excruciating headache overcame her. The lamp that he had just bashed against her head shattered into pieces. She tried to scream, but only muffled whispers entered the airwaves as the man stood over her with a blank face. He began to urinate over her body as she laid there in a daze and whimpered in agony.

"You thought I wouldn't find you? Huh? It wasn't an accident that I ran into you tonight at that bar. I have been looking for you for over a year. Now it's time to repay that debt. You took $400,000 from me. I want that back in blood . . . plus interest." The man walked to the corner and grabbed the iron that he had turned on when they entered the room an hour before.

So many thoughts raced through Draya's mind as she struggled to release herself from the tight handcuffs. *Why? Why did I do this to myself?* She heard steam gushing from the iron.

He pushed the button repeatedly, antagonizing her with the sounds of terror. He approached her and prepared to torture her for what she had done. He was about to cash in on his long-awaited revenge.

CHAPTER ONE

Four years earlier

DRAYA HURRIED AS SHE PULLED THE CLOTHES OUT OF THE DRYER. She briefly stopped to wipe the sweat from her brow. It was fifteen minutes after her shift was over and she had to hurry and finish up the laundry before the last bus ran for the night. She glanced at the clock on the wall and took a deep sigh. *I'm going to miss my damn bus,* she thought as she turned the knob on the dryer. She was instructed by Mrs. Harris to have all the clothes washed before her shift. Draya was in the laundry room of the mansion that sat in the hills of Novi, Michigan. She'd had the job for the last three months as a part-time housemaid. She hated being a maid, but it served as motivation for her, working in such a lavish home. It was the house she eventually wanted one day. It was by far the most glamorous house she had ever been inside of. It was something that she could never afford or even fathom staying in. There were marble floors everywhere and high-priced Andy Warhol paintings on the walls. Draya felt as if she was being teased the three days of the week she worked for the Harrises. Yet she liked the job because she got paid under the table. She had answered a newspaper advertisement to get the job and agreed to get paid cash, no paperwork involved. This was right up Draya's alley. She needed all of the money she could get and paying Uncle Sam threw a wrench in her program.

As she hurried to put away the towels that she had previously folded, she began doing a mental countdown. She had ten minutes to finish up and get out the door to walk to her bus stop just outside the suburban subdivision. As she hustled to the hallway closet, she heard the sounds of jazz playing loudly and grew nervous. She instantly knew that Mr. Harris was in the house, and that was a rare occasion. It seemed as if Mrs. Harris scheduled Draya to come in only when he wasn't there. Draya only recalled seeing him twice, and as she was putting the towels in the closet she glanced over to notice him standing there with his six-foot frame and dark-as-cocoa skin. He had on slacks and a dress shirt. His tie was loose around his neck and his cuff links were absent from his shirt. His broad shoulders and muscular build made him intimidating. His salt-and-pepper goatee displayed his late forties, but he wore his age well. Draya looked deeper and her eyes grew as big as golf balls when she saw him place stacks of money into a hidden compartment behind a painting. The security was in the fact that it was so inconspicuous. She realized that he hadn't seen her so she quickly returned down the hall to the laundry room. Her heart was beating fast as she began wondering about Mr. Harris, who she'd been told was a real estate investor.

He must not trust banks, she thought as she began to pull off her apron. At that moment, Mrs. Harris walked past the hall and did a double take. The six-foot-tall blond, blue-eyed fox stopped in her tracks. Mrs. Harris looked like a model straight out of a Victoria's Secret catalog. Draya was always slightly bothered by their interracial marriage. She felt like there was a shortage of successful black men and Mr. Harris had lowered her own odds by catching one.

"Oh, hey there. I thought you left already," the woman said as she checked her watch.

"I'm heading out now, Mrs. Harris," Draya answered, slipping on her jacket and giving her boss a nervous smile.

"Okay, well, hurry along. Mr. Harris and I are expecting a dinner guest," Mrs. Harris said as she put on a diamond earring. She was not a day older than twenty-six but had lucked out and gotten an older businessman to marry and spoil her. *Lucky her,* Draya thought to herself, putting on a fake smile and nodding her head. Mrs. Harris walked away briskly and announced, "Honey, I need you to run to the store and get wine for our guest," before fading into the rear of the home. "Oh, and Draya?" Mrs. Harris called out.

"Yes?" Draya responded.

"We're going out of town next Tuesday, so you can take the week off. I just need you here Monday morning to dust and give the house a good clean before we take off."

"Okay, so my only day of work for the week will be Monday?" Draya asked. Lord knows she needed those hours.

"Yes, that's correct."

Draya quickly gathered her purse and headed out. When she opened the front door, the winter's hawk hit her right in the face and the cold air sent a chill up her spine, so she zipped up her jacket. Michigan's winters were brutal and Draya was reminded of it every time she had to go outside these days. She pulled her knit hat from her pocket and slipped it over her head. Draya moved toward the bus stop, walking briskly with her head down to guard her face from the cold. She needed to get home to have a quick rest before going to her second job, a late-night shift at a local diner. Draya was twenty-five years old and had a good head on her shoulders. She had no kids, no man, and no drama. She took care of her seventeen-year-old knucklehead brother, filling the shoes of her mother who had died in a car accident seven years back. They had different fathers, who had both been missing in action their entire lives. So she and her brother June only had each other, which made their bond even stronger. They shared different last names, but their souls were closer than close. The typical story of young minorities in the economically declining city of Detroit.

Her brother wasn't an angel, but he was a good kid. So good that Draya knew he was probably their only ticket out of the ghetto.

As Draya made her way down the road, she heard a car approaching so she hugged the curb to get out of the way. She glanced back and noticed that the car had slowed. As it approached, the tinted driver's-side window came down and she saw the face of the man who employed her, Mr. Harris.

"It's freezing out here. How far do you have to go?" the man asked as he cringed from the cold. Draya had never heard him speak before. He had a deep baritone that was almost melodic.

"Oh, it's okay, Mr. Harris. My bus stop is just down the road," Draya replied, peering toward the end of the street.

"Where do you live?" Mr. Harris asked.

Draya paused, not wanting to reveal the area she lived in, which was smack-dab in the middle of the ghetto. "Eight Mile Road," she finally confessed, dropping her head in embarrassment.

"Hop in," he instructed, and hit the unlock button.

Draya was about to decline. Then she remembered the forty-five-minute bus ride, just to get a transfer. She managed a smile and walked over to the passenger side. As soon as she sat down, the warmth began to soothe her. His heated leather seats were like heaven and the smooth sounds of the Isley Brothers pumped through the speakers. The all-black Jaguar was luxurious and it felt like a spaceship to Draya. As she sunk into the seat, Mr. Harris pulled away.

"I really appreciate the ride," Draya said. She glanced over at the man and noticed his strong jawline and smooth black skin. He didn't answer her, just gave a quick grin and nodded his head. The ride was so comfortable and relaxing that before Draya knew it, they were at her exit. She gave him directions and soon he pulled up in front of her project building.

"Thanks," Draya said as she gathered her purse and exited the car. Once again Mr. Harris said nothing, he just nodded his head and smiled. Clearly he was a very quiet and modest man with a heart of pure gold. Draya knew that he was in unfamiliar territory. To a wealthy businessman, her projects must have seemed like a war zone and she understood that. So she hurried out of the car and watched as he pulled off.

Draya headed toward her building and noticed a young man standing by the door. A hoodie was pulled over his head and a scarf covered half his face, but Draya recognized his slim build and hazel eyes. Her brother June stood leaning against the door with his hands in his bubble down coat.

"Hey, sis. I see you un' caught a baller, huh?" he said as he gestured at the Jaguar that was turning off of the block.

"Boy, that is not . . ." Draya waved her hand in dismissal. "Why am I even explaining it to you?" She shook her head and moved toward him. June gave her his famous smile, which got her every time, flashing the small gap in his pearly white teeth. His baby face had no facial hair and in her eyes he was still the little brat running around the house looking up to her. June pecked her on the check, and just like always Draya smiled. He had his big sister under his thumb.

As she walked past, a small-framed woman wearing only a sweatshirt and jeans approached June. She placed some money in his hand and he slipped a rock of crack cocaine into hers. The transaction was swift and smooth, only lasting a couple of seconds. June scanned the block as the woman walked off.

Draya shook her head and went inside. She hated what her brother did, but she fully understood. He was a smart kid, and he had to survive. Draya's income could only support the rent and a couple household bills. She admired the fact that her seventeen-year-old brother pitched in and had the ambition to go out and get it.

Draya entered their small two-bedroom apartment and peeled off her jacket. She glanced at the clock and knew that she only had a brief period to relax before heading to her graveyard shift at the diner. She looked around the place and the thought of the big white house she had just left made this apartment seem that much more depressing.

She sat down at the kitchen table and noticed the stack of mail—mainly past-due bills with red lettering that only caused more stress. It didn't matter how much she made with her two jobs, it was never enough. As she flipped through them, she stopped and smiled when she saw the white envelope with her brother's name on it. It was a letter from the University of Michigan. It was the letter that she had been waiting on. She immediately ripped it open and read the first three lines, then smiled even wider. She screamed for her brother and ran toward the window that sat right above the spot where June was always standing.

"June! Come up quick!" she yelled in excitement. She had prayed to God for months for that particular letter and He had finally answered. June had been accepted to the college of his dreams and Draya felt a sense of deep accomplishment. Although they struggled and had gone through the loss of both parents, she had helped raise a pretty decent young man. He sold dope but he was a prisoner of circumstance. Yet through all his street dealings, he never missed one day of school and for that Draya felt proud. She was filled with joy, though the feeling quickly left as she thought about the tuition—the tuition they couldn't afford. Although June had been accepted, his 2.8 grade point average didn't warrant him any scholarships.

Draya heard the sound of the door opening and in walked June with his friend Blink, a kid about two years older than her brother. They were best friends and Blink had been responsible for introducing June to the drug game. Blink was small-time but everyone in the hood knew he was going to be the next big thing there—he had a boss mentality. June rushed in and began looking for the envelope. When Draya handed it to him, he quickly read it and gave her a half smile.

"This is cool, but how are we going to pay for it?" June asked. He had already made up his mind to go full-fledged into the drug game. The way he saw it, not going to school would give him more time to grind in the streets. By hook or crook, he was determined to come up.

"Well, you don't worry about that. You just prepare for this summer. You will be an official Michigan Wolverine. Trust that," Draya said as she put on a fake smile.

"I don't know how we going to do that," June replied. "All these jobs paying minimum wage and moving these eight balls ain't no real money."

"We need to hit a lick. Rob a plug a' something," Blink said, injecting himself into their conversation. He stepped forward with his hands in his pockets, a toothpick dangling from the left side of his mouth.

Draya looked at the kid in disgust, but then she began to think about what he had said. Flashes of Mr. Harris stuffing money into the secret compartment behind the painting popped into her head. And she remembered Mrs. Harris mentioning that they were going out of town for a week. Maybe all the stars *were* aligning for her to hit that lick. She knew

Blink's grimy ass would be down for the caper and Lord knows she needed the money. In those brief moments, she was already putting the play together in her mind. Nevertheless, she kept her thoughts to herself and snatched the letter back from June.

"I'ma get it," Draya stated as the wheels in her cluttered mind began to turn.

CHAPTER TWO

SOUNDS OF PLATES CLINKING AND THE ANCIENT HEATING SYSTEM filled the air. The small diner was dimly lit and the smell of fresh eggs and bacon flowed throughout the joint.

Draya, with her ponytail pulled neatly back and pearl earrings in her ears, was once again going through the motions, trying to get through her shift. As she wiped a table, the only thing she could think about was the stacks of opportunity she had seen Mr. Harris stuffing in his safe. She thought about the tuition that June would have to pay if he attended Michigan. She knew deep in her heart that if he stayed home and went to a community college, his chances of graduating would decrease. The environment that the city of Detroit offered would consume him.

Blink's words stuck in her head and she was truly thinking about setting the whole thing up. As her mind raced, she saw a familiar face walking in. He was about six two, brown skin, with a medium build. He wore a leather bomber jacket and a Gucci scarf was neatly wrapped around his neck. Crisp jeans and large Timberland boots made the outfit complete. Draya instantly grew nervous, as she always did when he walked in. His stride was unique and it seemed like he was marching to the beat of his own drum. His freshly cut Caesar and crisp black goatee enhanced his nearly perfect face. The only flaw was the healed three-inch cut along his jawline. The man sat in the back corner of the diner as he always did, and from across the room he locked eyes with Draya. She couldn't help but crack a smile, showing her pearly whites. It was her favorite customer.

She walked over to him with a menu in her hand, gently placed it in front of him, and pulled out her pad to take his order.

"Good morning," he said smoothly.

"Good morning, Cassidy," she replied as a big smile involuntarily crept onto her face.

"Why do you always call me by my full name? It's *Cass*," he said with a smirk and warm eyes.

"Well, I like Cassidy better. Now, what can I get you this morning?"

"I've been coming to this same diner at the same time for about . . . a good year. And you don't know what I want?" he asked as he slowly slid the menu back toward Draya.

"Eggs over easy, turkey sausage, and . . . Texas toast?"

"Bingo." He peeled off his coat and displayed a gold necklace with a diamond-encrusted Jesus piece hanging from it. They both shared a laugh and Draya started back to the kitchen when she felt a strong hand grab her wrist.

"Why do we play this game?" Cass asked.

"What game?" Draya countered, smiling from ear to ear.

"I've been coming here for a long time and we never get past this little exchange. I am feeling you and I know you feeling me. It's obvious, to say the least," Cass said with a charming, piercing stare.

"*I'm* feeling you?" Draya placed her hands on her hips. "How are you so sure?"

"Because you smile and turn red every time I come in here."

As if on cue, Draya's cheeks turned red. "Seems like you got it backward. You make sure you always sit in my section when you come in. If you ask me, I'd say *you* was chasing me," she shot back.

"Okay, you got me. I *am* chasing you. Let's stop playing . . . let me take you out sometime."

"I have been waiting for you to ask me that for a long time," Draya admitted as she smiled again and walked away.

Cass watched her waist sway from side to side. Her plump ass cheeks filled out her skirt and her large, thick legs were shining. Cass loved what he was seeing and was looking forward to learning more about this woman who he had been eyeing for months.

The sun was just coming up and Draya had one foot out the front door of the diner when she heard a horn beep. She shot her head in the direction of the pearl-white Range Rover parked to her left. She smiled: Cass had come back for her. She had given him her number a few hours before and told him what time she got off.

"What are you doing here?" Draya asked, grinning as she walked toward the truck.

"I couldn't wait. I wanted to kick it with you. Can I take you home?" Cass asked.

"Sure." She ducked her head into her collar to avoid the windchill, then walked over and jumped in the vehicle. "So, Mr. Cassidy, I never see you around here except for in the diner. Are you from here?"

Gripping the wood-grain steering wheel, Cass glanced over at Draya. "Nah, I'm from Cleveland. I just come here once a month to check on my uncle."

"You check on him the first of every month, huh?"

"I never miss. He practically raised me. Never had a father so he stepped in, feel me?" He rubbed his goatee with his free hand. "He's the only family I have left."

"You're a good nephew," Draya said. She felt cozy in his car but butterflies formed in her stomach as she tried to remain cool. She peered over at him and observed the way his jawline showed when he bit down on his teeth. He gave her a smile and pulled off.

Cass took her home and they sat in the parking lot for two hours . . . just talking about life. Draya was really feeling this mystery man named Cass. He had a sexy mystique and she was getting a good feeling about him. He was a great listener and seemed caring, but most of all . . . he was gangster. Draya was intrigued.

As Cass cruised the Detroit streets he smiled, thinking about how he was feeling Draya. He wondered what it would feel like to make love to her. Her body was enticing and she had such a pretty face. He quickly shook off the thought and got back to business. He had vowed to never get involved with any chick from Detroit. To him this trip was always about business. He only came to Detroit to get the shipment from his heroin connect. His uncle was his plug—the man was an underground legend in the city. Unstepped-on dog food, straight off the banana boat.

Every first of the month, Cass would come to the city and pay his uncle back for the previous shipment and pick up the new joints. It was a flawless system that they had going on. Cass was stationed in the next state over, in Cleveland, Ohio. He supplied the whole city and had a good operation set up.

Cass pulled onto Jefferson Avenue to one of his main trap spots in the city. It was a small house in the middle of a fairly quiet neighborhood. There were bars on each window and cameras at the front and the rear of the place. Cass's uncle had the local police wrapped around his finger, so the house was secured and free to operate. The only people Cass and his crew ever feared were the feds or stickup kids.

He hopped out and headed to the door, which had a steel gate on the front. Cass tapped in a rhythmic pattern to tell the patrons it was a known visitor. Seconds later, the door opened and a tall, dark brolic man appeared. He had a full beard, a nice neat cut, and an ice-cold stare, but he quickly smiled when he saw who stood in front of him.

"Cass, my nigga," the man said as he slapped palms with him.

As they moved into the midsize house, the smell of cooked crack filled the air and the latest Mobb Deep song pumped out of large speakers. This particular place was a half-and-half house, meaning you could buy crack *or* heroin. Cass looked around and smiled. Five young women sat at a table preparing the goods for sale. A girl stood in front of the stove working two pots, waiting for the powder coke to turn into crack rock, with a little help from baking soda. The operation was smooth and booming. Cass rubbed his hands together and nodded his head

in approval. Not one girl looked at him or acknowledged that he had entered the room. He loved it.
They were focused and straight about the business.
He turned back to the man who had opened the
door, still nodding his head in approval.

"You got this mu'fucka pumping, Gee," Cass
said. This was his head street general and as solid as
they came. He had been working the city for Cass for
years and was making a lot of money for himself too.

"No doubt," Gee replied, glancing at the girls
and nodding his head as well. Besides Cass's uncle,
who had been an important figure in the streets of
Detroit for years, Gee was the only person he dealt
with directly. Cass was like a ghost in Detroit. Niggas
within the city knew it was an out-of-towner coming
in and flooding the streets, but no one knew who he
was. Cass wouldn't have it any other way. He came
to town once a month, dropped the bag off, collected
his money from the previous trip, and left. The perfect hustle.

Cass motioned for Gee to follow him. He maneu-
vered through the front room and ended up in the
back. As soon as they walked in, the smell of weed hit
Cass's nose, and he heard money running through a

machine. He saw a tableful of cash and three hand-guns on top of it. He looked at the two young boys who were smoking while doing the count-up. Gee whistled to get the young boys' attention. When they looked up at him, he threw his head toward the door. Immediately they rose up and walked out, giving he and Cass privacy to handle business.

"So, how we looking this month?" Cass asked as he sat down at the table of money.

"We right on point. We almost out of the last joints. Those were a good batch, man. The ones with the scorpion stamp on them were pure as fuck," Gee answered, referring to the new fishscale cocaine that Cass had hit him with. Cass's uncle had a new supplier and the dope was so pure you could cut it three times and still have a strong product. It had the whole city on fire. They had finally got the pure shit in.

"Yeah, those scorpion joints are official. I'll tell Unc to keep those coming," Cass assured Gee, smiling slightly.

Gee smiled as well and went to the six-foot-tall safe that sat in the corner of the room. He put in a combination and the box opened, revealing a couple of stacked, plastic-wrapped squares with scorpion stamps in the middle of them. He reached in and grabbed a black book bag which contained about a quarter of a million dollars.

Just like every month, Cass would go visit his uncle and then head back home. Everything was always the same . . . But on this trip, he had more than business on his mind. He was still thinking about Draya.

He decided to stick around for a few more days. Maybe he could "bump into" Draya again. He smiled thinking about getting with her. There was something about her . . .

CHAPTER THREE

DRAYA STARED OUT OF THE WINDOW AS SHE RODE the transit bus through the streets of Detroit. The possibility of getting the money for her brother's tuition weighed heavy on her shoulders. She had lost so many loved ones to the streets—to drug addiction, prison, and death—and she was afraid for June. She had been strong and in control for so long, so now that she was helpless, it tugged at her heart heavily. She was never the grimy type but the images of Mr. Harris stuffing that safe wouldn't leave her brain.

Maybe I should *take that money. I need it more than him and I'm sure he has plenty more where that came from.* But how would she do it? That was the million-dollar question. She thought about all the cameras they had around the house. It would be almost impossible to take the money without incriminating herself. If Mr. Harris was a street cat, Draya would not think about taking it, for fear of the consequences. But the man was a square and the only thing he would do is call the police. Plus, she was sure he had insurance so it wouldn't hurt him. *Those damn cameras are everywhere except the bathrooms*, she thought as the bus pulled up to her stop.

She quickly shook off the notion and began to prepare for her overnight shift. Although she desperately wanted to get the money, it seemed impossible that she could get away with it. Draya stepped off the bus in front of the diner. When she walked in, the first person she saw was Cass. He was speaking with her manager toward the back of the diner. Draya wondered what were they talking about, but she would soon find out.

Silvia, a petite Mexican girl who also worked there, walked up to Draya with a grin. "You are one lucky girl," she whispered, carrying plates in both hands, and whisked right past her.

"What?" Draya replied. She focused back on Cass and her manager. She saw Cass slip something into the man's apron and then shake his hand. Cass turned and looked at Draya. Cass gave a rare smile and headed toward her.

"What's going on?" Draya asked, confused but half smiling.

"Come on, Ma. You going with me," Cass said slyly as he stood right in front of her. The fresh smell of cologne came off his garments, and his crisp goatee and jet-black Caesar instantly turned Draya on. Cass was all man . . . and everybody knew it.

"But I have to work." Draya started blushing heavily. All the other waitresses were looking at them. Half of them seemed happy for her and the other half were turning up their noses in spite.

"Nah, me and Hector have an understanding," Cass said. What Draya didn't know is that Hector had been on his uncle's payroll for years and that this very diner was a stash spot for their drug business. In fact, his uncle *owned* the place. Cass had also blessed Hector with two thousand dollars just for letting Draya take the night off.

Cass brushed past her and quietly whispered in her ear, "You coming or what?" Draya smiled broadly and looked over at Hector. Her manager nodded, giving her the go-ahead. Draya slowly shook her head in disbelief, feeling like a real-life Cinderella. Cass had pulled a boss-move and she was speechless. The only sound that escaped her lips was a nervous chuckle. Cass exited the diner and Draya wasn't far behind.

***

"Wow, this is beautiful," Draya said as she cuddled beside Cass while they watched the fire dance inside the massive fireplace.

He had driven her about three hours north of Detroit and they were staying in one of his uncle's cabins for the night. The wooden masterpiece was unlike anything Draya had ever seen. As soon as she stepped inside the cabin, the smell of pinewood invaded her nostrils and the shiny wooden floors amazed her. Draya was so impressed by the sexy rustic setting. It was spacious and seemed a world away from Detroit. Cass felt joy in seeing her react like a little child at a museum. He knew for sure at that moment that he wanted her.

Hours later they were settled on a bearskin rug about a foot from the gigantic fireplace. Draya was really feeling Cass. They talked and laughed, debating things like who was the best rapper, Jay-Z or Nas. It seemed as if they had known each other for years and everything flowed so naturally. They sipped champagne and shared a small joint of the finest California weed.

"What are your plans for life?" Cass asked as he puffed on the joint and passed it to her.

"My plans? What do you mean?" She took a puff of the joint before handing it back to Cass.

"Like, what is the one thing you want? What's your dream? Everybody has a dream."

Draya noticed that he looked at her different than other guys. It seemed as if he was looking into her soul rather than *at* her. "Uhm . . ." She tapped her cheek and peered up as if she was in deep thought. "Oh, I know!" she finally said.

"Okay, what is it?" Cass took another deep puff of the slow-burning joint.

"I want to open my own diner," Draya said, slightly embarrassed by her small goal.

"A diner? That's dope. I can see you running a spot."

"Fa real?"

"Fa real, fa real," he said smoothly, holding the smoke in his lungs. He threw what was left of the joint into the fire.

"I never did anything like this before," Draya said, glancing up at Cass who was now downing the last of the champagne from the bottle.

"Like what?"

"Like this, ya know." Draya sat up and gazed

deep into Cass's eyes. "No one has ever treated me this nice."

"Well, I'm not everyone else. I'm Cassidy Long," he said confidently.

"Is that right? Mr. Cassidy Long, huh?"

"The one and only," he replied. "I think you are one of the most beautifulest girls in the world. You have that *real* beauty, that natural beauty. Every time I see you, you have your hair pulled back, no makeup on. I get to see the real you, unfiltered. Your beauty is pure."

Draya blushed again and swept the hair from her face. She loved Cass's approach. He had an honest vibe and seemed so real. He was 100 percent and she could feel it.

Draya hadn't really thought about it until then but she hadn't been with a man in over a year. She was so busy working and taking care of her brother, she hadn't been making time for herself. She looked at Cass's dark chocolate skin and felt her love button begin to throb—she was getting aroused. So much so that she began to squirm. Cass leaned in and pressed his lips against hers and it seemed like they were melting into each other. Their hands were all over each other as they passionately French-kissed in front of the flickering fire. She loved his strong hands and the way he handled her. It was rough and aggressive but with care. He slid his hand down into her jeans and touched her love box.

Cass was surprised the instant he got to his destination. Her panties were already soaked. It caused a chain reaction, because his rod began to grow rock hard as all of the blood flowed to the peak of his mountain. Cass had been anticipating this very moment for a while. He had been determined to get into the mind and body of the beautiful woman who now sat before him. Cass slowly inserted his finger into Draya's wetness, causing her to close her eyes as she held onto his muscular arms. Cass loved her response and knew just what to do. He slowly began to rub her clitoris with his thumb as he placed his lips on her earlobe. "This is going to be mine," he whispered as he plunged deeper. Draya slowly nodded her head, and Cass moved his lips down and gently kissed her neck while carefully and strategically finger-popping her. He took his time; the world was on his watch and he was in total control.

Cass took his hand out of her pants and stood

up. The dim light from the fire made him seem like a God as Draya looked at him in admiration. He pulled his polo shirt over his head and tossed it onto the floor, revealing his tattooed body and ripped physique, never taking his eyes off Draya. She licked her lips involuntarily, waiting to taste him. She was yearning for him; her love button had never been so swollen in her life. She was ready for his entry.

Cass unbuckled his pants and they dropped to the floor, exposing his white Polo boxers that tightly hugged him and put his large package on display. Draya pulled off her shirt and then her bra. Cass watched carefully and began to slowly stroke his rod through his drawers. Draya undressed completely, revealing her plump buttocks. Her thick thighs and bowlegged stance had Cass enticed. She stood up and looked into his eyes. He then pulled off his boxers and exposed himself. Draya peeked down and saw the vein bulging from his erect penis and almost lost her breath. She reached over and began stroking and it felt like a rock in her hand as she tugged on the curved masterpiece. She dropped to her knees and took him into her mouth and cupped his sack as she gave him slow, deep fellatio. Cass put his hand on the back of Draya's head and then threw his own head back in pleasure; her hot mouth was driving him crazy. The alcohol and the newness of being in his company had Draya in complete bliss.

Cass felt himself peaking, so he stepped back. Now it was her turn. He grabbed a pillow from the nearby couch and placed it on the wooden floor. He laid down and rested his head on the fluffy pillow while Draya sat and watched. Without saying a word, he signaled with his index finger for her to come to him. Draya smiled, wiped her mouth, and crawled over. She lifted one leg and straddled his ripped body. Her leaking box dripped onto his pelvis area as they locked eyes. Cass swiftly pulled her over and she was now on his face, lining her love box with his mouth. Draya closed her eyes and placed her hands on the floor, draping over him. She slowly began to grind against him. Cass grabbed Draya's buttocks as he moved his tongue in circular motions and gently sucked on her button. She ground harder and Cass began to move his tongue in overdrive. Draya felt a tingle down below and began to speed up her pace. Masterfully and with perfect timing, Cass pushed Draya down to ride on his tool. He was now inside of her and they began to make passionate love until both of them had numerous orgasmic explosions. It was beautiful . . . it was the beginning of something special . . . they could both feel the deep connection.

The night ended with both of them completely satisfied and out of energy. They laid there and talked for hours until the sun came up, and they both agreed it was one of the best nights of their lives. The mystery man had Draya open . . . wide open.

CHAPTER FOUR

DRAYA SMILED AS SHE LOOKED DOWN AT THE TEXT FROM CASS. It was a simple *Good morning, pretty girl* on her screen, but it made her grin from ear to ear. It had been days since she shared the great experience with Cass up north at the cabin, yet the intimate memory made her blush every single time she thought of him. It was Saturday morning and she had the day off. She decided to spend the day relaxing and putting a plan together for the upcoming week. She heard chatter coming from the front room, including an unfamiliar voice. She crept to her door and peeked into the living room and was surprised at what she saw. Blink, June, and some younger guy she didn't know were sitting there counting money.

"What's going on here?" Draya asked as she came into full view with her arms crossed. All eyes shot to her.

"What's good, Draya?" Blink said, smiling at her and wrapping a rubber band around the knot of money he was holding.

"Morning, sis." June was smiling with überexcitement. He stood up and held a fistful of money in the air. "Look at the lick we just hit!" he yelled.

"What's going on? Where y'all get this money from?" Draya took another step forward to get a better view of the table.

"Blink set the whole thing up. We hit old man Johnson's spot," June said as he flicked through the bills. Mr. Johnson had been running numbers in the streets since the early '80s. She never liked his old pervert ass, so she grinned. But she quickly wiped the smile off her face when she thought about the potential backlash.

"How much di—" Draya started her sentence, but was cut off by Blink.

"You talk too much, lil' nigga," he said to June, before snatching the money out of his hand.

June, always playing the little-brother role with Blink, tried to explain himself: "Man, she's cool. She not going to say nothing."

"How much y'all make?" Draya asked as she picked up a wad of money from the table.

"About ten racks," June said proudly. "He was loaded."

"So let me get this right: y'all ran up in a spot, risk y'all lives, and only getting what . . . three thousand apiece?" Draya shook her head. They were chasing small money that would be gone in a month's time. She walked back into her room in disgust. It was one more reason why she had to get June off to college and out of the projects.

Blink's eyes were on Draya's ass the whole way. He'd always had a crush on her, though he knew he didn't stand a chance with her until he got his paper up. He was determined to get a taste of her one day.

Draya entered her room and closed the door, still thinking about how dumb they looked. *Three thousand dollars! That ain't shit. Not enough to . . .* She stopped in her tracks and it was like a lightbulb had popped on in her mind. She knew how she would hit the Harrises. She could see it so clearly now. *I got it.* Blink had a reputation in the hood as a jack boy as well as a seller. Draya knew that he was the perfect guy for the job she had in mind. She was about to go for the gusto. If Blink agreed, she would hit the biggest score of her life. One that would set her up for a long time and send June to college.

* * *

Days had passed and Draya was once again cleaning at the Harrises' house. But it wasn't just an ordinary day. It was the day she had picked for the robbery. She had gone over the plan with Blink and June for what seemed like the millionth time. She knew that because the house had cameras, it would prove that she had nothing to do with the robbery. She had the perfect plan. She continued to dust the mantel in the front, just as she would any other day. Her heart pumped as she tried to keep calm. She glanced toward the rear of the house and wondered why Mr. and Mrs. Harris were taking so long. *Are they still leaving? Did they notice my nervousness?* These and other questions raced through Draya's mind as she tried to look as normal as possible.

June and Blink sat in a Chevy Blazer parked five blocks away from the big white house. They waited patiently for Draya's call so they could put their plan in motion. A chrome .45 sat in Blink's lap, along with a ski mask. June also had a gun and a ski mask, and he rubbed his hands together thinking about the big caper they were about to pull off.

"I hope your sister is sure about what she saw,"

Blink said as he moved the toothpick around his mouth with his tongue.

"She say it's a sure thing," June replied confidently. He looked at the big shiny gun in Blink's lap and began to get nervous. Despite hitting old man Johnson, robbery wasn't his game and he had never shot a gun in his life. In fact, he was secretly scared of guns, though he would never tell this to Blink. Blink was the more aggressive of the two and June had been following his lead for years. "That mu'fucka's not loaded, right?" June said.

"Nah, not a single bullet in this pretty bitch." Blink held it up, pointed it to nothing in particular, and squinted one eye for aim. He was lying through his teeth, but he didn't want June to get more anxious than he already was. Blink always kept his clip full— it was a way of life and he wasn't about to change up just because June's sister was involved.

"Okay, cool. I just don't want any mistakes, ya know?" June said as he wiped away the small beads of sweat that were beginning to appear on his forehead.

Blink had been thinking a lot about all of the money that Draya had described and he already had plans for it. It was on.

* * *

Mr. Harris watched as his beautiful half-naked wife hustled around the room packing her luggage. He sat back in the corner and smoked a cigar while enjoying the view. He had been packed up for two days; he never liked to rush, so he was always well prepared. He had scheduled a trip to Nicaragua for business and decided to take his wife. He glanced down at his watch and noticed that they were running a bit late. Their flight was scheduled to leave in about two hours and he knew that they should have already been out the door and headed toward Detroit Metropolitan Airport.

"Honey, we have to hurry," he said as he held his head back and blew cigar smoke into the atmosphere. Clark Harris loved his life. He was financially stable, he had a young, beautiful, blue-eyed goddess as a wife, and he lived with no regrets. He watched her long legs that connected to petite buttocks and instantly got aroused.

"Katie," he said as he grabbed himself, rubbing through his Armani slacks.

Mrs. Harris was so focused on trying to gather things from the closet and stuff them into her luggage, she didn't hear him. Mr. Harris reached over and put out his cigar in his custom ashtray and called for her again.

She had her passport in her hand and was about to put it in her purse, but stopped and looked over at her husband. She tossed her passport onto the bed and took off her lace bra, exposing her perky-watermelon breasts. Clark had a certain gaze in his eyes when he was in the mood. The creamy Nicara-guan smoke danced in the air as he stared down his wife intensely.

She knew that facial expression all too well. She smiled, grabbed the red pair of Louboutins from her bag, and quickly slipped them onto her feet. She slowly walked over to him, still grinning. *Click, clack, click, clack.* The sound of her heels hitting the hard-wood floor echoed throughout the room as she made her way to her man like a lioness to her prey.

"We have to make this quick," she acknowledged before dropping to her knees. She unbuckled his belt and pulled out his semihard pole. She began sucking . . . and sucking with precision. She used both hands and slowly twisted them; she knew just what to do to drive him crazy. Loud slurping noises filled the air as

Clark threw his head back in pleasure. Her gigantic double-D silicone breasts sat front and center and her nipples were hot pink and stood erect—pointing directly toward him. Clark reached down and began to pinch her nipples, admiring his fifty-thousand-dollar investment. He'd bought her the best set of tits money could buy and didn't regret one dime of it. Clark watched as she went wild on his manhood and he stretched his legs out and tensed up as he felt a huge orgasm approaching. Katie knew what was coming so she sucked harder and faster. Just when he was about to explode, she sat up and grabbed both of her breasts to give him a target to shoot his load on. And that's exactly what he did, releasing a grunt and jerking uncontrollably as he climaxed. Katie placed her hands on his knees and used them as a crutch to stand to her feet.

"You're going to make us late!" she said, smiling.

"I know, I know. I couldn't resist it, honey, I couldn't," he said, smiling too. Needless to say, they were way behind schedule.

Draya looked down at her watch and saw that the Harrises were running late. They were supposed to have left more than twenty minutes earlier. She began to get nervous and headed to the bathroom, where there were no cameras, so she could tell Blink that it was a no-go.

"Come on, come on, pick up," she whispered impatiently, tapping her foot as she listened to the phone ring.

"Hello," Blink said, finally picking up on the fourth ring.

"Yo, don't come! They are still here," she whispered, pacing back and forth. She wished she had told them to show up an hour later and was now for sure pulling the plug.

"Nah, fuck that. I need that paper. We coming in that mu'fucka, if they in there or not," Blink responded, and hung up. He then turned his cell off so Draya couldn't stop what he already had set in his mind. The way Draya had explained it to him, it was the caper of a lifetime and he wasn't going to let it pass him by. He was going in that big white house with or without Draya's blessing.

"Oh my God! No! Do not fucking come!" Draya whispered harshly into the phone, trying to keep her voice down, not noticing that he had already hung up. "Blink! Blink!" She finally looked at her cell screen, then hurried and dialed the number again, only to get his voice mail. She tried to call June, but got the same result. Voice mail.

Fuck! she thought and ground her teeth. She flushed the toilet just in case the couple could hear her and stepped out of the bathroom. She then spied the heels of Mrs. Harris coming down the hall.

"Okay, Draya, we're about to head out. Finish your shift and make sure you turn on the alarm before you leave. Your pay for the week is on the counter in the white envelope," Mrs. Harris said as she rolled her luggage right past Draya. She headed out the door to load the car and Draya picked up the duster and tried to look as busy as possible so she could avoid eye contact with them. She didn't want them to notice her anxiety and tip them off to anything.

Seconds later, Mr. Harris came walking across the room with his luggage. Draya dusted the mantel, and for some reason she looked over at Mr. Harris. They locked eyes and for the first time she saw the man smile. It made her heart drop because she knew she was about to do him dirty.

Moments later Draya heard the door lock behind him and she breathed a sigh of relief, knowing she had just dodged a bullet. She made her way to the front window and saw them pulling off. It was time to put her plan into motion. She knew the cameras were rolling so she tried to act as normal as possible.

Okay, okay, be calm, she thought to herself and opened the front door to check the mail. She did this so she could intentionally leave it unlocked for Blink.

Once outside, she pulled out her phone to see if she had any new texts. It was ten thirty a.m., the minute when Blink was supposed to arrive. As she walked toward the mailbox at the end of the driveway, she saw Blink and June coming toward the house. She quickly slid the mail out of the box and hurried back inside.

Blink gripped the gun inside of his hoodie, anxious to see how much was stashed in that secret compartment. He was so excited that his dick was hard, and he already had plans for his portion of the money. Whatever was in there, he was putting it right back into the streets. He was trying to come up and had big cocaine dreams that he was determined to realize. Blink glanced over at June who was even more nervous; he didn't like the way June ran his mouth. He had taken a mental note after the Johnson robbery and vowed to never do a caper with June again. But this opportunity was too good to resist.

"You ready to do this?" Blink said as they approached the front door.

"No doubt," June answered, pulling out the little .22-caliber gun and slipping the ski mask down over his face. Blink followed suit and pulled out his own gun and mask.

Just as promised the door was unlocked and they rushed in with their guns up. When Blink came in he saw Draya placing the mail on the table and moved toward her with his gun pointed.

"Oh my God!" Draya yelled as she threw her hands up, putting on a Oscar-worthy performance for the rolling security cameras. "Please don't kill me!"

"Don't fucking move!" Blink shouted before rushing toward her and putting the gun to her forehead. Blink then hit Draya over the head with the butt of his gun out of instinct. He was totally locked in now and there was no turning him off. June looked on in confusion and saw his sister fall to the floor and hold her head in agony.

"Yo, where is the stash!" he demanded, still pointing the gun to her head.

June rushed over to him and grabbed his arm harshly. He leaned over and aggressively whispered in Blink's ear, "What the fuck are you doing?"

"Getting money!" Blink shot back and yanked away from June. "Search the house!"

Draya laid on the floor trying to gather herself from the blow to her head. *What the fuck is he doing?* Fear overcame her soul—the hit had caught her completely off guard and she had to remind herself that it was a setup. After she shook off the stars she was seeing, she could faintly hear Blink's voice again.

"I said, where is the stash?" he repeated through clenched teeth. He bent down and grabbed Draya's hair and pulled her to her feet.

"Down the hall to the right," she whispered, covering her face. June was now running through each room looking for valuables.

All of a sudden the front door opened and in walked Mrs. Harris. She had forgotten her passport on the bed in their bedroom; her sexual rendezvous with her husband had distracted her and she'd left it behind. Mrs. Harris's head was down as she searched inside her purse, so she didn't notice at first that a robbery was taking place.

Draya's heart dropped when she saw Mrs. Harris's face. The woman gasped when she finally noticed a masked man holding Draya by the hair.

Blink, with no hesitation, squeezed his trigger. Two loud thuds erupted and a small spark emerged from the gun's barrel. The hollow-point bullets entered Mrs. Harris's chest, causing two maroon-colored circles to emerge on her white peacoat. Mrs. Harris collapsed to the floor and gripped her chest in pain.

"Nooooooo!" Draya yelled at the top of her lungs. She broke from Blink's grasp and rushed to the aid of Mrs. Harris. Blood poured out of her chest and her eyes were rolling in the back of her head. "What did you do? Why! Why?" she shouted. Her hands were shaking frantically.

Mr. Harris burst inside the house in a frenzy; he had heard the gunshots from the car. He had a gun in hand from his glove compartment, but before he could even raise it, Blink fired another shot, hitting him in the thigh.

Mr. Harris went flying back and dropped the gun

in the process. "Aghhh!" he screamed as he gripped his leg.

Draya's body went numb. Everything was happening so quickly. June came running downstairs with his mask off. He had panicked and removed it after he heard the shots and commotion.

"What the fuck are you doing, man?" June yelled when he saw the bloody couple on the floor.

Blink was at the point of no return and had a killer look in his eyes as he blocked out all of the yells and cries. He walked up to Mr. Harris who was on the ground grimacing. The older man looked across the room to where his gun had landed and began to crawl toward it, but he couldn't feel his entire left leg. Blink stood over him as blood squirted out of the wound and he breathed heavily, obviously in excruciating pain.

"No, Blink. No!" Draya screamed.

She immediately realized she had said his name. The plan had now gone totally awry, and Draya knew that her life would never be the same. She watched as the helpless Mr. Harris rolled around in complete agony. She glanced down at Mrs. Harris and saw her blue eyes staring into space; her life had already left her body. When Mr. Harris flopped over to his wife, Draya stood up and put her hands over her mouth. She shook her head wildly and cried herself a river. "I'm sorry. I'm so sorry," is all she could utter as she watched the man weep over his dead wife.

Mr. Harris fought through the pain and focused on his wife. He ran his hand over her eyes and closed them. He kissed her and then closed his own eyes. He was bracing himself for impact. "I love you," he whispered, and rested his head on her chest.

Blink placed the gun on the back of the man's head and pulled the trigger.

CHAPTER FIVE

T EARS STREAMED DOWN DRAYA'S FACE as she tried to wipe down everything in the house that she could have possibly touched. Blink was in the storage room, retrieving the tape. Draya told him that they used the same tape and rerecorded on it daily. Also, there was no official record of them ever having employed Draya so she was trying to disconnect all ties. Meanwhile, June's true colors emerged as he sat on the couch in a daze. He had never seen a dead body and sat frozen in fear while Draya and Blink moved around the house.

"Got it!" Blink yelled when he emerged from the back, holding a tape. "Let's head to that painting." He looked over at June and shook his head in disbelief. *I knew that lil' nigga didn't have any heart*, he thought, grinning at the bitch that had come out of June.

Draya brushed away her tears and knew that she had to remain calm so she wouldn't make any more mistakes. She wanted to curse at Blink, but she would have to do that later. She had to adapt to her current situation: cover her tracks and get the money.

"Follow me," she said, and they headed to the spacious master bedroom in back. Blink rubbed his hands together as soon as he entered the luxurious room. He went right to the dresser and noticed the extensive Rolex collection there in plain view. Mr. Harris had everything from platinum to gold bands, modest to diamond-encrusted faces. Easily half a million worth of watches. Blink grabbed a pillow and Mrs. Harris's passport fell onto the floor. He yanked the pillow out of its case and used it as a knapsack, dumping the Rolex tray in, already thinking about where he would pawn them off.

Bingo, he thought. *This is bigger than I imagined. We hit a honeypot.* He glanced back at Draya who was examining the painting, trying to pry it open. For some reason it wouldn't budge; it seemed to be bolted to the wall.

"What's the problem?" Blink asked. He walked over to the painting and studied it closely. It was a nude oil painting of Mrs. Harris. Blink inspected every curve and color, and finally saw something . . . an inconsistency. On one of Mrs. Harris's nipples, the texture looked different. He touched the spot and instantly knew it was a hidden button. He pressed it hard and voilà . . . the painting swung open like a door, exposing an open vault behind it. Blink winked at Draya; in front of him appeared every dope boy's dream. His knees began to buckle. The safe was about a foot deep and full of both money and bricks of cocaine. "What the fuck?"

Although Draya was still shaken by the murders that had just taken place, the sight of all the money and drugs changed the game.

Blink's dick started to get hard all over again as he pulled out one of the cocaine bricks and studied it. There was a stamp of a scorpion front and center. He had just hit the jackpot. "Let's load up!" he announced with a smile.

Draya, June, and Blink sat at the kitchen table and looked on in awe. They had been there for six hours and had counted the money three times. It was exactly $330,000 and fifty bricks of raw, unadulterated cocaine. Blink knew that this grade of dope could go for $30,000 per brick on the street. That totalled up to another $1.5 million.

"I still can't believe you did that crazy shit," Draya said in disgust.

Blink was unfazed. He had just come up and wasn't worried about what he'd done to achieve it. "Look, Draya, are we going to talk about old shit or talk about splitting this money up?" He put his hand on top of one of the scorpion-stamped bricks.

Draya simply shook her head. "Okay, we've got $330,000 here. That's . . ." She pushed a hundred-dollar stack toward Blink, pulled a stack toward herself, and scooted one over to June. "A hundred thousand apiece. It's thirty left—that's mine. The bricks . . . You and I can split those," she said without hesitation.

"Yo, that's not even," Blink frowned.

"Well, it was my lick—my rules," Draya replied.

Blink nodded his head, not wanting to complain. After all, she was forgetting about the Rolexes he had in the pillowcase.

"What about me? What about *my* bricks?" June asked, pouting.

"*Your* bricks? Nigga, you going to school. You are done with the streets. Matter of fact . . ." Draya reached into his pile and grabbed a stack of bills. "This is for your school tuition. I'll hold onto this for you." She was taking full control and wasn't trying to hear any suggestions from either of the two youngsters before her.

"You shouldn't be getting shit the way you bitched up in there," Blink said, smiling as he began dumping his portion of the bricks and money into a black garbage bag that sat at his feet.

"Don't do that." Draya shot a menacing look over at Blink.

"Whatever," Blink said before standing up, and rubbed his hands together. He was ready to leave; he had a lot of things planned. He grabbed the bag and grunted while picking it up, then headed toward the door, leaving Draya and her brother alone at the table.

"Yo, Blink," Draya said just before he reached the door.

"Yeah?" Blink played with the toothpick in his mouth, switching it from side to side with his tongue.

"Stay away from June. This is the last time we should see each other."

Blink chuckled and nodded his head in agreement as he opened the door and exited the apartment. As soon as he was gone, Draya closed her eyes and took a deep breath. She put her hand on her chest and exhaled. She had been very worried that Blink was going to put a bullet in her and June's heads and take the money all for himself. She glanced at June, who was smiling while recounting his share.

"Lock that door," Draya instructed. June jumped up and did as she asked. He was smiling so hard that Draya realized he didn't really understand what they had just done. Murder was a serious crime and they had killed a very important man. She had never known Mr. Harris was in the drug business—and that's what scared her most. Somebody would come looking for their product.

"You don't get it, do you, Julian?" she said, calling him by his government name. "You don't even realize what's going on, do you? We aren't going to do anything! We are going to live our lives like we have been. You are going to college this summer and we are going to forget this ever happened. You hear me?" Draya pointed her finger at her brother.

He had never seen his sister so angry, so he conceded and nodded his head.

"We are going to lay low and get you ready for college just like Mom and Dad wanted. After that, we will never see this city again. But we have to get away from this apartment. It's too hot. We're sitting ducks. Blink doesn't have any sense, and honestly, I do not trust him." Draya had a plan and she was going to stick to it.

CHAPTER SIX

DRAYA HAD A LOT ON HER MIND as she wiped down a table at the diner. She was on the last hour of her graveyard shift and was on pins and needles. Although she had a lot of money and tons of drugs, she didn't want to do anything differently. She thought at any minute police would come rushing in and arrest her for murder. It had been two days and there wasn't a second that went by that she didn't think about it. Draya had put her brother and herself in downtown Detroit; they were staying at the MGM Grand hotel to lay low. She couldn't wait until the school year was over so June would graduate and go to college. She had convinced him to take summer classes so he could leave immediately. His graduation was one month away. *Just one month*, she whispered to herself as she cleared the dishes from an empty table. She was planning on leaving the city, the diner, and her past life forever.

Just as she completed the thought, in walked

Cass. Instantly, a wave of guilt came over Draya. He had been texting her, but there had been so much going on that she hadn't responded to him. Now, however, she thought about their passionate night up north and her spirits lifted. He sat down in the same area he did every time he came in. Draya put the dishes away and headed toward Cass. She grabbed her pad out of her apron and approached him with a smile.

"Hey, handsome," she greeted.

"Hey, beautiful," he replied with a half smile before looking away.

Draya noticed the difference in his demeanor. She also noticed it wasn't around the first of the month, the usual time he came into town. "Ay, what are you doing here anyway? I usually don't see you in town this time of month."

"I've been trying to call you," Cass said calmly.

"Yeah, things have been crazy for me lately. I came down with a little cold over the last couple days. I'm fine now, though." She was starting to get butterflies in her stomach—she wasn't a good liar and hoped he didn't notice.

"Oh, okay. I'm glad you doing better." He pulled

out his phone and checked for text messages. "Just give me the regular."

"No problem, sweetie," Draya said and placed her hand on the nape of his neck. "Are you okay?"

"Yeah, I'm cool. Just going through some shit right now." He finally looked up at her with his dreamy eyes. "Can we talk?" He placed his hand on top of hers.

"Sure, I'm off in about thirty minutes," she replied, glancing down at her watch.

Draya and Cass sat silently in his truck outside of the diner. It was an awkward silence and Draya wondered what was going on with him.

"My uncle got murdered the other day," he started. "They went in and killed him and his wife before robbing him. That man meant the world to me. He was the only family I had." A single tear crept down his cheek. He stared forward as he clenched his teeth and the muscles flexed along his jawline.

Draya's heart dropped and it seemed as if all of her blood had escaped her face. She waited for a reaction, but got none. Her knees began to tremble and she quickly placed her hands on them to stop them.

"Oh my God, Cass, are you okay? Who would do something like that?" Her voice was shaky and she was scared to death. Did he know it was because of her? *That's the uncle he was always coming to see?* Draya couldn't believe the odds of this happening.

"We don't know who did it. Nobody has a clue. Unc moved so careful. He was so low-key. I don't know who would do something like this. He was a good man. A damn good man."

"Oh my goodness. Baby, I'm so sorry. I'm here for you," Draya said, trying to comfort and read Cass.

"Yeah, I'm good. I just have to get ready for the funeral this weekend. I need to get away or I'ma go crazy. Let's get away for a couple nights. Let's go back up north," Cass suggested, gripping the steering wheel tightly.

"Of course I will, baby," Draya said, not knowing what else to say. Then she began to wonder if Cass was playing possum and knew that she had been the mastermind behind the whole setup. *What the fuck! What did I get myself into? I cannot believe this shit is happening. I have to remain calm. I can't act differently in the slightest.* She had already made up her mind that this would be her last time with Cass. It was too close . . . too dangerous.

* * *

Draya looked over at Cass who was sleeping next to her. They had talked all night at the cabin and he'd told her great stories about his uncle—they had been closer than close. He had explained to her that his uncle had been a retired drug kingpin and only did business to keep Cass's own operation alive. Cass felt the robbery was all his fault and was taking it real hard. Every time he mentioned how good and noble his uncle had been, it was like a sharp dagger straight to Draya's heart.

Cass had really opened up to her and she could tell that she had gained his trust. He also talked about retaliation, and Draya tried to squeeze as much information out of him as she could to see if he had any leads. But he had none.

Draya slipped out of the bed, grabbed her cell phone from the nightstand, and stepped into the living room. She dialed her brother to check up on him. She had decided that when she returned home, she would pack their shit up and leave town right away. Things were getting too crazy and too close to home. *Maybe Atlanta for a while*, she thought. She had some high school friends who had moved down there.

"Hello," June said as he browsed jewelry at a local jeweler.

"Hey, what going on?"

"Oh, nothing. Just at the library," he lied, as the jeweler handed him a heavy gold rope. He slipped it around his neck and looked at himself in a mirror the jeweler held up and smiled, all while holding the phone to his ear.

"Okay. Well, we might leave quicker than planned. We need to get out of this city for a while," she said, glancing over her shoulder to make sure she was still alone.

"Yeah, okay. Whatever you want to do, sis," June said, not really paying attention to what she was saying.

"Okay. Keep a low profile and please stay away from Blink."

"I got you, sis," June responded, pulling out a wad of money to pay for his new piece. "Listen, I gotta go. Talk to you later, sis. Love you."

June hung up and looked at Blink who was also getting a necklace and slapped hands with him. They were about to shine and wanted the whole city to see.

"I love you too," Draya said, not realizing the call was already over.

"Good morning," Cass greeted from the doorway, startling Draya. His naked ripped body was a work of art. His half-erect penis was on full display.

"Hey you," she responded, and tucked her phone in her bra. Draya was nervous but quickly calmed down when he gave her a warm smile. Her eyes drifted down and she liked what she saw. She loved the way Cass was so comfortable with his body and didn't mind being completely naked in front of her. Even when his thick penis was half hard it was a sight to behold. Draya walked over to him, stood on her tiptoes, and gave him a kiss.

"Thanks," Cass said.

"For what?"

"For being here with me. I really needed you and you were there. I appreciate you." Draya could still see the pain in his eyes. She so badly wished she could reverse time and just erase what she had done. However, she knew there was no possible way to do that. Sadness overcame her when she remembered that after this brief trip, she could never see Cass again. She had finally met a guy who she was feeling and she couldn't have him. They were two peas in a pod, battling their own dilemmas—ironically, from the same unfortunate event.

CHAPTER SEVEN

BLINK AND JUNE CRUISED THROUGH THE CITY STREETS in a brand-new Beemer, fresh off the lot. Blink had just copped the black-on-black joint with white seats. He was feeling like an overnight celebrity and was glad to finally be in a position of power. He ended up pawning the watches for $50,000 even—only a fraction of their real value—and still had his share of the bricks from the robbery. He knew exactly where to unload them and headed to the trap spot to give his big homey an offer he couldn't refuse. Blink was high off life plus a gram of the powder that he had taken from one of the bricks—it was the purest coke he had ever sniffed. He had on a fresh leather Pelle Pelle and wood-grain-and-gold Cartier glasses on his face, with a wooden toothpick dangling from his mouth. A freshly lined haircut and a pocketful of money made him feel like Tony Montana. He glanced over at June who was admiring his own gold chain and bobbing his head to the music blasting from the speakers. June was loving the attention they got in the mall earlier and the feeling of money in his pocket. He was definitely catching the vapors.

Blink pulled up to a house that his big homey ran and instructed June to wait in the car. He was going to try to unload the bricks at a wholesale price, to make a quick profit. Blink lifted the armrest and grabbed the small baggie full of coke. He sprinkled a little between his index finger and thumb, then dipped his head and used his nose as a vacuum. He quickly threw his head back to prevent his nose from running. After a couple of seconds he closed his eyes as he felt the total euphoria.

Blink looked over at June and held up the baggie. "Here, take a bump," he offered.

June had never done coke and had no desire to, even though he sometimes slung it in their project. However, he felt obligated to prove that he wasn't soft. He was still embarrassed by the fact that he had frozen during the Harris robbery and wanted so badly to prove himself to Blink. So June grabbed the bag and mimicked what he saw Blink do: he poured a small snow hill between his index finger and thumb and then sniffed it up.

"Slow down, homey! Take it easy," Blink laughed.

June threw his head back and felt an instant rush. He was in new territory. "Fuck . . ." he said under his breath as the drugs hit him like a ton of bricks.

"Yeah, nigga," Blink said, "you tried to be superman on your first go-around. Yo ass going to be stuck. Like I told you, stay here. I'm going to run in here real quick." He reached in the backseat and grabbed the duffle bag holding the bricks.

June watched Blink exit the car and turned up the volume of the music so that he could zone out. His rush came almost immediately, and he began to fidget and squirm. For no apparent reason, he opened the glove box. He saw a small cassette and suddenly knew what it was. *What the fuck?* He grabbed the tape that could put all of them in prison for life. *He was supposed to destroy this,* June thought as he examined it. He shook his head in disbelief and then stuck the tape in his pocket so that he could burn it later.

Blink, meanwhile, walked up to the trap spot and reached his hand through the armored guard door. He gave it a knock and seconds later a man with an emotionless stare answered.

"What's good, Gee?" Blink said.

"What up, lil' nigga? What you need?" the man asked, looking Blink up and down, noticing that he was fresher than usual.

Blink held up the bag and smiled. "I want to talk business."

Gee opened the door and let Blink in. "You want to talk business, huh?" He looked at the bag with skepticism. "Let's step in the back, lil' homey." Gee threw his head toward the rear of the spot.

"No doubt," Blink said confidently, moving the toothpick around in his mouth. They made their way to the back and Blink didn't waste any time. "I think I got something that you might be interested in, big homey."

"Let me see what you got," Gee said, peering down at the bag at Blink's feet.

Blink kneeled down and began to pull out the bricks of cocaine. He stacked a couple of them on the table and smiled, feeling proud. He knew that Gee would be very interested in what he was offering. "I know you can do magic with these. I will let them go for the low too. This that grade-A shit. Make me a offer." Blink crossed his arms and smiled.

Gee picked up one of the bricks and smiled too.

Blink began to rub his hands together, knowing that he had a sell in the bag.

"Yo, where did you get these?" Gee asked as he examined the brick.

"I hit a quick lick. Nothing major. It was light work," Blink said cockily.

"Oh yeah. Light work, huh?" Gee smiled again and nodded his head. Almost instantly, he caught Blink across the face with a right hook. Blink crumpled to the ground and held his jawbone, which felt like it had been disconnected. Gee quickly reached into the small of his back and pulled out an all-black Glock .40. He pressed it to Blink's forehead.

"You have to be the dumbest mu'fucka of all time or have balls the size of melons. You bring me scorpion-stamped bricks? The same ones that was taken from my people's uncle?" Gee said and whistled, signaling for his young boys in the front room to come join them. "These are *our* bricks, nigga! You stupid mu'fucka! . . . Take this nigga in the basement! Did he come alone?" Gee asked his henchmen.

"Nah, somebody's in the car," one of them answered.

"Drag his ass in too. It's about to get real ugly. Yo,

get Cass on the phone. He ain't going to believe this shit," Gee said, just before giving Blink a thunderous kick to the midsection, making him fold like a lawn chair.

Draya sat across from Cass as they ate brunch together. They had just shared a quick and much-needed lovemaking session. She noticed that Cass's joy was short-lived and he had wrinkles on his forehead that weren't going away. She could tell a lot was on his mind. She had even more on her mind and hated the fact that their relationship could be no more. Cass had no idea that this would be the last time they made love. Just as Draya was about to say something, Cass's phone began to buzz. He wiped his hands and mouth with a napkin before picking up the cell.

"Hello?" he answered, then listened carefully and remained quiet. It was an uncomfortable silence as Cass sat there soaking in what was being told to him.

Draya peeked at him and tried to ear hustle, but she couldn't make out what the other person was saying. The only thing she knew was that it was a man's voice. She grew anxious and feared her cover was being blown. Draya was preparing for the worst and her palms began to sweat. Her nerves were starting to get the best of her.

After a minute of not saying anything, Cass finally spoke: "Good. I'll see you this evening to take care of that." He disconnected the call and a smile came over his face as he began eating again. He chuckled to himself and shook his head. Draya felt relieved. *Whew*, she thought, realizing that she was just being paranoid.

"What has you smiling? Musta been good news," Draya said.

"You really want to know?" Cass asked as his smile grew even bigger.

"Of course," she answered.

"They found the two niggas that killed my uncle."

Draya's heart stopped. She felt like she couldn't breathe. "Wha . . . what?"

"Yeah, they found out who did it. Can you believe they fell right in our lap? Blew one of their brains out and the other one got away. We gon' find him though. It's only a matter of time. We'll find him."

Draya felt the urge to cry. She thought about

June and hoped to God he was the one who got away. She had butterflies in her stomach and suddenly wanted to vomit. She got up and rushed to the sink, letting out a small scream as her breakfast came up. Cass swiftly got up and rubbed her back until she stopped heaving.

"I'm so sorry, baby. I'm talking reckless and letting you into my world. You not supposed to hear things like that."

Draya wiped her mouth and breathed heavily. "Sorry, Cass. I have a weak stomach."

"No, I'm sorry." He ran his hand through her hair and kissed her forehead. "Are you okay?"

"I'm fine. I just need to gather myself." She hurried to the bathroom, closed and locked the door behind her. She took out her cell and dialed June's number. While the phone was ringing she prayed that she would hear her brother's voice on the other end.

"Please God, please God . . . let June pick up," Draya whispered as tears began to fall down her cheek. She got the voice mail so she hung up and tried again. Once again . . . voice mail. Draya's whole world crumbled as she assumed the worst. She

JaQUAVIS COLEMAN | INFAMOUS

scrolled down her phone contacts and called Blink. After a couple of rings, she heard a lot of commotion and then Blink, out of breath, answered.

"They killed him! They killed June, Draya!"

Draya dropped her phone and covered her mouth as she began to cry her heart out—all while trying not to make a sound and tip-off Cass. She had just lost her only family. She had just lost her baby brother. She was broken. Karma was real and she was getting a firsthand lesson.

Blink hung up the phone and bent down, resting his hands on his knees. He had run almost ten blocks from Gee's trap house. When the goons had gone to the car to retrieve June, he made a break for it out of the rear of the house and got away. He had wanted to go back for June but knew he was outgunned and outnumbered. He breathed heavily as he hit himself in the head, thinking how stupid he was to get himself in this situation. The bad move cost a young man his life. "Fuuuuck!" he yelled in the air and staggered down the street. He dipped between some houses, knowing that he had to get out the area, and quick.

* * *

Cass glanced over his shoulder, making sure Draya was still in the bathroom. He put on a coat and went outside to get some privacy—Gee was on the other end of his phone.

"I want to make a statement," Cass instructed. "Hang his body in the middle of downtown, so everyone can see. He's going to be our commercial to the streets. Niggas goin' to pay for what they did to my uncle. Put a fifty thousand–dollar tag on the other kid's head. I want him brought to me on a platter." Even though Gee put five bullets into the back of the kid's head, that wasn't enough. Cass wanted the whole city to feel his wrath for what they did to his uncle. Now, his only focus was to do the other kid the same way.

That, and build his relationship with Draya. He truly believed that he had found someone special. She was helping to ease his pain and he respected that. Little did he know . . . she had *created* his pain.

CHAPTER EIGHT

TOTAL PANDEMONIUM WERE THE ONLY WORDS TO DESCRIBE the streets of Detroit. It was the most gloomy week for the city in recent memory. A well-respected OG was put to rest and days after a young man hung from a streetlight with a bullet-riddled body. The entire city was on pins and needles and the local officials were in a frenzy trying to hold everything together. The media had a field day with the murders and tried to connect the two, but no one knew the true story; no one except Blink and Draya.

Draya had to have a secret funeral that was by invite only, a closed-casket service. Only classmates of June and childhood friends could attend. Draya pleaded with the newspapers not to mention her name or those of any other relatives. She told them it was out of respect for the family, but in reality she didn't want her cover blown, which might give her the same fate as her baby brother. Draya also asked the police to park outside the funeral, just to be safe. They agreed and posted two officers.

Draya went over the scenario again and thought about what she could have done differently. However, it was a mental exercise in futility because there was no bringing her Junebug back. She thanked the Lord for her decision to ask Mrs. Harris to pay her under the table, so there was no record of her ever being involved with the Harris family. Draya was a wreck and no amount of money could heal her pain, not even the substantial amount of drugs and dead presidents she had in the back of her rental car. She would have traded it all away to get a reset button on her life.

Draya sat in the front pew of the funeral home, puffy-eyed and sniffling, as she stared at the closed wooden casket in front of her. The funeral had been over for two hours but she hadn't moved. She just sat there and cried and asked June to forgive her for putting the plan together that took his life. As she wept, she felt a hand on her shoulder. Someone had crept behind her without her knowing. Draya instantly went into her inner coat pocket and pulled out the small .22-caliber pistol that she had purchased that same morning at a pawnshop. She turned and pointed the gun at the man behind her and staring right back

was Blink. He had on a black hood and shades, trying to be as low-key as possible.

"Yo, chill, it's me," he said as he snatched off his
shades.

Draya, with tears running down her face, lowered her weapon and took a deep breath of relief.
"Damn, Blink, you can't sneak up on me like that."
She tucked the gun back inside her inner coat pocket.
She didn't know how to feel about Blink; she didn't
know if she should be mad at him or what. The only
thing that she did know for sure was that he was the
only one who understood her whole truth, and that
they were in the same boat.

"I can't even look at my man like this," he said,
peering at the casket and shaking his head in disbelief. He walked up to the casket and placed his hand
on the shiny wood. He bowed his head and quietly
said his last goodbye to his partner. Seeing Blink gen-
uinely hurt slightly reduced Draya's skepticism about
his loyalty. But she didn't know that Blink was a master manipulator and that his only thoughts at that
moment were on the bricks that Draya still had. He
had lost his by default to Gee and he wanted to get
his hands on Draya's so he could set up out of town

and out of harm's way. Every dope boy in Detroit was looking for him and he knew that he was on fire within the city limits.

Blink managed to squeeze a tear out, and seeing that, Draya broke down even more. She stood up and embraced him. She could feel the steel on his waist and knew that he could relate to her. She felt that someone would come and blow her brains out any second. She kept seeing flashes of her brother's body with the bullet holes and the rope marks around his neck. Identifying his body had been the absolute hardest thing she'd ever done. Every local news channel had her brother's name in the headline and the streets were talking. She couldn't escape the pain anywhere she turned.

"They didn't have to do him like that," Draya said, resting her head on Blink's chest.

Blink put his hand on the back of her head and stroked her hair. He had a warm feeling as he looked down at the beautiful woman. He'd always had a crush on her but she would never give him the time of day. In his demented mind, he began to imagine her naked. While she cried her eyes out and looked to him for comfort, he was thinking about having his ass in the air. Blink saw that she was vulnerable, so he went for it.

"Listen, I have to make sure you all right. We all we got. We have to get out the city," Blink said, and put a finger under her chin so she could look into his "watery" eyes. He was laying it on thick and was going to see how far he could go. "From what I'm hearing, the old guy was the brick man and was well connected. Connections with the Mafia—and they coming for the people responsible. On top of that, his nephew put money on my head. It won't be long before they find out June had a sister. We have . . . to . . . go," he concluded, putting emphasis on each word.

With June gone, Draya had no solid plans and didn't know what to do. All she knew was that she needed protection and that Blink was a shooter. She needed him, so she nodded her head in agreement.

"You still got them bricks?" Blink asked as he threw his arm around her and headed toward the rear of the church.

After they buried June, they were on the first thing smoking out of Detroit. Blink already had a place in mind.

* * *

A little over year later Blink and Draya had settled in Atlanta, Georgia. They were living in a nice, modest condo in a quiet suburban area. Blink had already grown larger than life in the Atlanta drug scene. He had taken Draya's bricks and cut them, doubling the profit. The product was still strong, and was the best cocaine that Atlanta had seen in years. Blink quickly became the go-to guy and as his pockets grew, his street fame did as well.

The tides had turned completely. Blink had convinced Draya to move in with him temporarily in Atlanta, so he could protect her from potential retaliation. However, he had also become more than just a roommate to her. One drunken night, Blink had sexed Draya and she quickly discovered that he was gifted in the bedroom. His rugged approach and chocolate member had Draya's nose completely open—she had never orgasmed so much in her life. But with that and her newfound weed habit, she was becoming dependent on Blink. He slowly milked her of her money to the point that even if she wanted to leave, she couldn't because she no longer had the funds to do so. Cass was a distant memory to her at that point.

Draya stood in the bathroom one morning wearing a luxurious terry-cloth robe. She leaned into the sink and splashed water on her face. When she looked into the mirror she hated what she saw. Her left eye was blackened and sore from the previous night's argument with Blink. He had accused of her of cheating when she came back later than expected from a spa outing. She had taken more time than he felt fit for a pampering session and the black eye was the end result of an hour-long shouting match. And it wasn't the first time Blink had been physically abusive to her. His anger was uncontrollable from time to time and Draya got the shit end of the stick when he lashed out.

She walked into their bedroom which had all-new furniture that she had custom ordered. She loved the condo, but hated being there. Aside from the sex, there was no love inside of that home and Draya felt trapped. She looked at the bed and saw a powder-blue Tiffany's box with a chocolate bow neatly wrapped around it. There was a greeting card on top of it, propped up perfectly. Her name was handwritten on the front. "An I'm-sorry gift," she said aloud as she walked over to it and opened the card. It simply read, *I'm sorry, baby. I love you.*

He had left earlier that morning and must have crept in to deliver the gift while she was in the shower. Draya unwrapped the bow and opened the box to take a look inside. It was the most beautiful necklace that Draya had ever seen. She picked it up and grinned as she admired it, then placed it back in the box and headed to the walk-in closet. She had all types of mink coats and red-bottom designer heels. Yet she couldn't enjoy them because every time she saw an expensive item that Blink had purchased for her, a memory of a beating went along with it. Draya thought often about leaving, but with no savings and no connections, she was stuck. She was more unhappy than she had ever been. It seemed as if her life had stopped when her brother got brutally murdered. She tiptoed around the house and tried to stay out of the way of Blink's sporadic mood swings. She just wanted out. For some reason, on that day Cass popped into her thoughts.

I wonder what could have been, she said to herself as she looked through the hanging clothes. But then the thought that he had been involved in her brother's death killed the notion. Out of nowhere, she got a wave of courage and began ripping her clothes off the hangers. She pulled her Louis Vuitton suitcase from the shelf and walked over to the bed. She threw it on the bed and began to stuff inside as many clothes and shoes as she could. "I'm sick and tired of this shit!" she yelled. "I'm leaving and never looking back!" She dug out a shoe box from the corner of the closet and opened it. There was nearly three thousand dollars inside and it was all she had left to her name. It wasn't much, but she would take her chances—anything was better than being a prisoner in her own home.

Once she had stuffed the bag to its capacity, she got dressed. She didn't care about leaving everything else behind in the condo. The only thing she grabbed was the picture of her brother from her bedside table.

Blink was weaving in and out of traffic and kept checking his rearview. He was sure he was being followed. He had just dropped off ten kilos to one of his faithful Atlanta customers and was on his way back home. He had noticed the Chevy Impala behind him a few miles back, so he began to change lanes to see if it would follow . . . and it did.

He had a feeling that the feds had been watching him lately, and this was only confirmation. He looked in his rearview again and saw a marked car creep behind him. He figured he was about to get pulled over, though he had no immediate worries since he had just relieved himself of the drugs, and the sale had been on consignment so he didn't have much cash on him. There was only a couple grand in his pocket. Blink, at that point, was just waiting for them to hit the lights and pull him over. He thought about his honeypot; he had nearly half a million in drug money in his safe at home. So Blink picked up the phone and called Draya.

Draya heard her phone ring as she was headed out the door for good. She couldn't wait to talk to Blink; she would let him know everything that was on her chest and tell him to kiss her ass goodbye.

"Hello," she answered as she stood by the front door.

"Look, it's a 911. I got the cops on my ass. I'm sure they're going to hit the house as soon as they get a search warrant."

"What?"

"Listen! Go to the den and look in the closet. Built into the floor, there's a safe. The combo is 11-28-34. Write this down . . . 11-28-34." Blink saw lights flashing behind him and hurried to give Draya all the instructions. "It's just under half a million in there. Take one hundred bands to my lawyer and tell him to come get me. Pronto! Then get out of the house!" Blink instructed and hung up.

Draya couldn't believe what she had just heard. *He just made this too easy.* She felt an adrenaline rush and a burst of happiness as she dropped her bags and ran to the den. "11-28-34," she repeated aloud. She had never known about the safe and always wondered where Blink kept his dirty money. She rushed to the closet and hastily pulled away all of Blink's clothes that were scattered everywhere . . . and there was the safe built right into the floor.

"Bingo!" she said, and began to turn the dial. "11 . . . 28 . . . 34." And just as promised, it was full of money. She grabbed one of Blink's duffle bags in the closet and filled it up with C-notes. She hurried, like her life depended on it. She was expecting the feds to burst in at any moment. But she knew that if she got out of there with the money, she would vanish forever.

Fuck Blink and his lawyer, she thought as she pulled out the final stack and tossed it in the bag. She then zipped up the heavy bag and stood. She slung it over her shoulder and shuffled out of the room.

"Karma's a bitch," she said aloud, smiling as she exited the house.

CHAPTER NINE
THE AFTERMATH

Three years later

DRAYA'S LIFE HAD REALLY TURNED AROUND. She was finally happy with herself and her position. She had opened a small diner in a small city in Georgia, Macon to be exact. She called it *Julian's* after her late brother. She hadn't heard from Blink and didn't want to. She had been laying low in Macon and was in a great space in her life. The money she took from Blink helped fund her restaurant and she had purchased a small duplex which was giving her a nice return on her investment. Draya had blossomed into a great businesswoman after the horrible curveball life had pitched her. She always thought about Blink coming for her. She wasn't sure if he was in jail or not, but it was no longer her concern. She figured it was a fair exchange after everything he had put her through. That life was long gone and behind her.

Draya sat in the back of her diner and went over the weekly budget. She took a break and finally lifted her eyes from her work. She looked around and smiled at her small business running so smoothly. She felt safe. Cops ate free, so there were always local police there. She smiled and nodded her head as she looked at the menu and saw her late brother's name at the top of it. She really felt proud to keep his legacy alive somewhat. She was planning on attending school the coming fall. Draya had everything under control.

She had been working so hard, she'd forgotten it was her birthday. However, her staff didn't forget. A wave of rhythmic claps filled the air as her five-member crew came out singing happy birthday, taking Draya by surprise. Then a small cake was placed in front of her with a candle directly in the middle of it. A single flame had never to so beautiful in Draya's eyes.

"Oh my God. Thanks, you guys," Draya said as she admired the beaming faces around her. She felt loved. She blew out her candle and a round of applause erupted.

"Boss lady, we need to celebrate! We were planning on going to the casino tonight. If you're not do-ing anything, you should come with us," one of the girls suggested.

"Yeah, it would be fun!" another girl added.

Draya hadn't gone out and enjoyed herself since she'd moved to Macon. She had been so focused on her business and staying low-key, she never even con-sidered it. "You know what . . . that's a good idea. Let's do it!" she said, deciding to spend her thirtieth birthday amongst friends.

Draya sat in the corner of the bar. All five girls from Julian's were there and it had been a great night. The bar was attached to the local casino and hotel and Draya had been drinking all night, having more fun than she'd had in years. Bottles were coming and the music was live. Wearing an all-black dress and black red-bottoms, Draya was the star of the show. At thirty, she could still compete with the younger girls.

"Hey, girls, I have to pee. Where's the restroom?" Draya asked.

One of the girls pointed across the room. "Over there," she said.

"I'll be right back," Draya announced. Once she

stood up, she felt the liquor hit her and she wobbled slightly. She maintained her balance and pulled her slightly rising dress down, while doing a shimmy dance. Draya made her way to the restroom and handled her business, but when she came out, her heart skipped a beat. She saw the face of a man who she thought she would never see again. He stood there expressionless and he moved the pick around his mouth with his tongue.

"Long time no see," Blink greeted, standing there against the wall as if he had no worries in the world.

Draya was at a loss for words and she felt her knees wobble again. Fear overtook her body as she stared at the man she had stolen money from. Blink slowly walked up on her and she had no idea what he might do.

Blink finally cracked a smile and hugged her. "I missed you, girl." He rocked her back and forth in his arms. "Where did you go?" he asked as he gently let go of her and peered into her eyes.

"I had to leave town. Feds were coming and I slipped out of the back without them seeing me," Draya lied. "I didn't know what to do. I was so scared, Blink."

"Oh my goodness. My baby. I am so sorry I put you in harm's way. I'm just glad you didn't get involved in the case. I'm so happy you got away. You got the money, right?"

"No, Blink. I didn't have time. I had to run."

"Damn, so you didn't hit the safe?" he asked with a confused look on his face.

"Nah, I didn't have time. It all happened so fast." She tried to read Blink to see if he was buying her story. His face didn't reveal a trace of anger.

"It's all good. That was short paper. I got that back tenfold after they released me. I'm just glad they didn't get you." Blink took both of her hands in his with a look of genuine happiness.

This made Draya relax a little. *He's really buying this shit.* "What are you doing here?" she asked, trying to make light of the situation.

"I come past here a lot when I'm shooting moves. This is my route to the money. Got tired on my way home and decided to stop for the night. I hate driving late, especially if I'm tired," he explained. He softly cupped her face in his hands. "I know I had anger issues in the past, but I'm sorry now."

Draya didn't know what to think. It was as if she

was looking at a different man. Blink leaned in to kiss her and when she started to protest, his tongue ended up on her neck.

"Ooh, that feels so good," Draya said as she closed her eyes and began to think about their great lovemaking. Her clitoris slowly grew erect and her panties were getting wet from the thought of him inside her again. "No, Blink, no," she whispered, but that didn't stop him; he gently pushed her against the wall.

His hand went up her dress and he moved her panties to the side, then slipped two fingers inside of her, all while kissing her neck passionately. A small moan escaped Draya's lips and her whole body began to tingle. Blink remembered that moan as if he'd heard it yesterday; he knew that he had her open. As he fingered her slowly, his manhood began to grow. He pressed up against Draya even closer, so that she could feel what was in his jeans. They kissed as Blink played with her right in the hallway of the bar, not caring who saw them.

"I love you. I missed that pussy. I want you," Blink whispered while licking her earlobe.

"Oh, Blink," Draya sighed as she ground against

him. She hadn't felt a man in so long and the large amount of liquor in her system had her ready to explode.

"I have a room upstairs at the hotel. Let's make love," he said.

Draya nodded her head with lustful eyes. She wanted him so bad. It seemed like everything that she had gone through with him had just flown out the window.

They burst into the hotel room, and Blink began taking off Draya's dress, exposing her tight, shapely body. He peeled off her clothing while sloppily kissing her. Within seconds they were both naked on the king-size bed.

Hard as a rock, Blink slid into Draya's dripping-wet box and both of them moaned at the same time as they fell into pleasure island. Draya arched her back and dug her nails deep into the man's chocolate muscular back.

They proceeded to make love and Draya tried to remain calm, but she kept thinking about how crazy Blink had once been. She had already made up her mind that she would lead him on as if they were getting back together, then leave him in the dust just like she did before. Now she couldn't wait until their little meeting was over so she could get ghost on him. She would play the part well until she got her chance to leave.

"You were amazing, Daddy. I am so glad I ran into you." She looked around the luxury suite and noticed a slightly opened duffle bag sitting on the floor. She could just glimpse some plastic-wrapped cocaine bricks stacked neatly inside of it and she chuckled to herself. *Why did I even come out tonight? No growth,* she thought as she shook her head. "I see not a lot has changed since the last time I saw you. You still getting it in, huh?" she said as she sat up and began tying her hair into a ponytail.

"You know it, Ma. Don't shit stop," Blink replied from the bathroom.

Draya put on a fake smile and giggled nervously. She still wondered if he knew that she had robbed him. *That's the way the game goes sometimes. I had to get mine,* she thought, trying to make herself feel better about what she'd done. *If a nigga get caught slipping, it's his own fault.*

She flipped onto her stomach and grabbed her

phone from the nightstand. As she began scrolling through her contacts, she heard the water turn off in the bathroom and then Blink's footsteps approaching her. She wiggled her plump butt cheeks, knowing that he was watching, and smiled and giggled while still focusing on her phone.

She felt his warm hands begin to rub on her back and then heard his deep voice: "It's been a long time, baby." He took her phone from her and set it aside, then gently pulled her hands behind her back. His demand for her attention turned Draya on and made her smile even wider. She could feel his growing warm shaft resting on her leg. That sensation alone made her clitoris begin to jump in anticipation of round two. She started moving her body like a snake, in a circular motion, causing friction between the bed and her clitoris as she closed her eyes in total bliss. With her arms still behind her back, it made everything more exotic and she was loving every second of it.

"Please put it in again, Daddy," she urged with exaggerated enthusiasm.

Blink remained silent and prepared to give her the business. The cold handcuffs startled Draya as they were slapped across her wrists. Almost instantly, a bandanna was slipped between her lips and he tied it behind her head so tightly that it hurt.

"I've been waiting to catch you for over a year, you grimy bitch," he said as Draya began to squirm like a wet fish. It all happened so fast that she hadn't seen it coming. Something crashed down on the back of her skull, causing her whole world to shake up. Her vision went blurry and the most excruciating headache overcame her. The lamp that he had just bashed against her head shattered into pieces. She tried to scream, but only muffled whispers entered the airwaves as Blink stood over her with a blank face. He began to urinate over her body as she laid there in a daze and whimpered in agony.

"You thought I wouldn't find you? Huh? It wasn't an accident that I ran into you tonight at that bar. I have been looking for you for over a year now. Now it's time to repay that debt. You took $400,000 from me. I want that back in blood . . . plus interest." The man walked to the corner and grabbed the iron that he had turned on when they entered the room an hour before.

So many thoughts raced through Draya's mind

as she struggled to release herself from the tight handcuffs. *Why? Why did I do this to myself?* She heard steam gushing from the iron.

He pushed the button repeatedly, causing the sounds of terror to antagonize her. He approached her and prepared to torture her for what she had done. He was about to cash in on his long-awaited revenge.

As he was about to place the iron against her back, there was a knock at the door.

"Room servas," said a man with a heavy Mexican accent. Then another knock. "Room servas," he said again.

"What the fuck?" Blink said quietly between clenched teeth. He was ready to do a number on Draya and the pesty-ass room service was interfering. Blink didn't want to take the chance of someone coming in, so he had to say something. "I'm fine. Please go away," he called out as nice as he could.

Draya tried to scream, but her voice was too muffled. Blink threw a cover over her and stepped to the door. He heard the same voice and knock again. As soon as he slightly cracked the door open, the force from a kick sent him flying back.

In walked Cass . . .

Cass closed the door and pulled out his chrome .45 with a silencer on its tip. He pointed it directly at Blink. "I've been looking for you, my G," he said calmly, as if they were old friends. Cass saw a body squirming under the covers and he quickly yanked them off to find Draya lying there in terror. He locked eyes with her and whispered, "It's okay, I got you."

Without hesitation, Cass walked up on Blink and put the gun to his head. "Did you think I wasn't going to find you?"

"Listen, I got money. Let's work this out," Blink begged as he put both of his hands in front of him.

"Fuck ya money!" Cass screamed, something he rarely did. The beast was coming out of him. "You killed my family. Now it's time to pay what you owe. But no money can take care of your tab. I need your life." He looked the man directly in the eye and put two bullets in his head, rocking him to sleep forever. Blood and brain matter splattered all over the wall as Blink's body went limp.

Draya squirmed and cried in terror; she knew she would be next. Cass sat down on the bed and tried to run his hand through Draya's hair, but she flinched in fear. He freed her mouth and grabbed the handcuff keys from a side table to free her. Draya pushed the covers off and began crying uncontrollably. She wasn't ready to die. Cass noticed how afraid she was and that her eyes wouldn't leave his gun.

"Relax, Ma. I'm not here to hurt you," he said as he tucked his gun inside of his waist.

Draya glanced over at Blink's lifeless body and all the blood that was sprayed everywhere. It was a horrific scene and she felt disembodied. "Please, please don't kill me," she begged, waiting for him to make his move.

"I'm not going to kill you. I know what happened. I know your brother was a part of the robbery and murder but you had nothing to do with that. You had no control over what he and this mu'fucka did. I have no issue with you. I'm sorry for what happened to your brother but he did something that had consequences. If it matters, I had nothing to do with his murder. My uncle was loved by a lot of people. The streets did that . . . not me," Cass lied as he tried to comfort her and put her at ease. He placed his hand on her foot. "I need to get you out of here. You have to listen to me, okay? . . . Trust me, I'm not going to hurt you. I just want to get you out of here. I got who I came here for. I've been tracking him for years and I finally got him. That's all I wanted. The bloodshed stops here."

He doesn't know that I set the whole thing up, Draya thought. She studied his face and saw no malice in his eyes.

"We have to get out of here. Did you touch anything?" Cass asked, looking around.

"No, I don't think so," Draya said between sniffles.

"Okay, good." Cass stood up and saw her panties, shoes, and dress on the floor. He picked them up and handed them to her. He pulled a small towel from his back pocket and wiped down the doorknob and lock. "Hurry up and let me take you home."

Draya got dressed and Cass pulled off his leather coat and put it over her shoulders. He knew they had limited time. He had paid an inside guy to kill the cameras for an hour so he could get Blink.

Draya's mind was gone. She couldn't think straight as they made their way through the hallways and out of the casino. She just wanted to go home. Her fearful days were over. Blink was dead and Cass didn't know she was involved, so she had nothing to run from anymore. When she thought about it like that, she felt a sense of liberation.

Cass insisted he would drop her off at home. He walked her to his Range Rover and, like a gentleman, he opened the door for her. After she got in, he entered the driver's side and cranked the engine. Draya let out a big sigh of relief as she threw her head back on the headrest.

"I'm so sorry about your uncle," Draya said, meaning every word sincerely.

Cass rubbed her hair and whispered, "It's okay. Just sit back, let me take you home."

It's finally over . . . it's finally over, Draya thought as she closed her eyes.

Cass grabbed a CD from his armrest and popped it in. Draya expected to hear music, but an image popped up on his in-dash television screen instead.

"Check out this movie," Cass said calmly.

Draya looked down at the screen and began to breathe heavily. It was the surveillance tape of the botched robbery. She watched herself in action: Mrs. Harris appeared on the screen and her body dropped after Blink let off a couple rounds. Seconds later, Mr. Harris appeared and his murder replayed. Draya's body froze in fear; she put her hand over her mouth and the tears began to flow—tears of guilt and agony.

Just when Draya took her eyes off the screen and looked over at Cass, a man emerged from the back-seat and threw a rope around her neck. It was Gee, Cass's right-hand man. He pulled the rope tightly while Draya kicked and clawed, but it didn't matter. Cass had a menacing stare on his face as he watched Draya struggle for her life, trying to slip her fingers between the rope and her neck. Her entire airflow was blocked. Her eyes were as big as golf balls when she looked into Cass's eyes.

"My man found this in your brother's pocket before he killed him. It told the whole story—you set my uncle up," Cass said as hate filled his heart and a devilish scowl appeared on his face. He watched Draya clawing at him, then slapped her hand away while Gee pulled and pulled with all his might with his feet on the back of the seat. "I have been waiting for Blink to lead me to you for years. I wanted to kill y'all together. It was a debt to pay. Now you're paying it . . . in blood."

Tears rolled down Draya's face as blood clots began to form in the whites of her eyes. Her lips turned purplish and she felt her life slipping away. Cass turned around now—he could no longer take watching it. However, he knew it had to be done. What had gone on in that infamous white house was cold-blooded and he had to avenge the death of the only man who ever showed him love unconditionally.

"*You* did this to you," he whispered, looking straight ahead and clenching the muscles in his jaw.

As the last word came out of his mouth, Draya's jerking movements ceased. It was quiet inside the car and the only thing he could hear was Gee's deep breathing. Gee kept pulling for several seconds after she stopped struggling, just to make sure the job was done. When he slowly unleashed his grip Draya's body slumped forward in the passenger seat, her life-less eyes staring into space.

She would feel no more pain. She was now in a space where she no longer had to live in fear. She could finally reunite with her brother. Karma had finally come back for Draya. The world has a strange way of making things even in life. You just can't outrun karma. Every action has a reaction and no bad deed goes unpunished.

Until next time . . .

The End

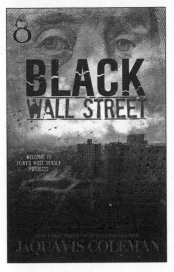